Brady Brady
and the MVP

Written by Mary Shaw

Illustrated by Chuck Temple

PUBLISHED BY
BRADY BRADY INC.

Published in Canada in 2004 by

Brady Brady Inc.
P.O. Box 367
Waterloo, Ontario
Canada
N2J 4A4

Canadian Cataloguing in Publication Data

ISBN 0-9735557-7-7

Brady Brady wins the MVP and learns a valuable lesson about
good sportsmanship.

Mixed Sources
Product group from well-managed
forests, controlled sources and
recycled wood or fibre
www.fsc.org Cert no. SW-COC-003049
© 1996 Forest Stewardship Council
FSC

Printed and bound in Canada

Keep adding to your Brady Brady book collection! Other titles include **Brady Brady and the:**

- **Great Rink**
- **Runaway Goalie**
- **Singing Tree**
- **Super Skater**
- **Big Mistake**

- **Twirling Torpedo**
- **Most Important Game**
- **Great Exchange**
- **Puck on the Pond**
- **Cranky Kicker**

- **B Team**

Brady was always the first Icehog player at the rink.
He liked to get there early so he could high-five his teammates as they walked into the dressing room.

The last, and loudest Icehog to arrive was Kev.

At first, the Icehogs were concerned when Kev showed up after everyone else all the time. They thought that maybe he didn't take his hockey, or his team, seriously.

But each time Kev came bounding through the door with a smile as big as the North Pole, they knew it was just his way of letting everyone know he had arrived.

There wasn't anyone prouder of being an Icehog.

At practices, Kev drove the coach *crrraaazy*! — especially when he talked with his mouth guard in. With a wave, Kev would holler, "Eh Oach!" each time he skated by the bench.

Often, he would remind the coach that he didn't want to sweat too much during practice because "he was saving his energy for games."

This was when the coach would usually make him do an extra lap.

Brady found it amazing that Kev could talk as much as he did and still manage to put his equipment on correctly. Well, except for the time Kev forgot to take his skate guards off and fell in a heap as soon as he touched the ice.

Kev didn't miss a beat. He leapt to his feet and waved to the crowd to let them know that he was okay.

At the start of each game, Kev would skate over to the refs, introduce himself, and chat awhile. A few times, the ref had to skate Kev over to his bench so that they could get the game started on time!

When Kev finally took his spot on the bench,
the cheerleading began.

Always standing, Kev would yell to his teammates,
"Let's go Icehogs! Skate hard! Nice pass! Great job!"

He didn't just save the chit chat for his teammates.
His favorite thing to do was to race up the ice beside an opposing
player and try to distract him.

Pointing up to the seats, Kev would say, "Hey, isn't that your granny in the stands?"

The player always looked up and always missed the pass.

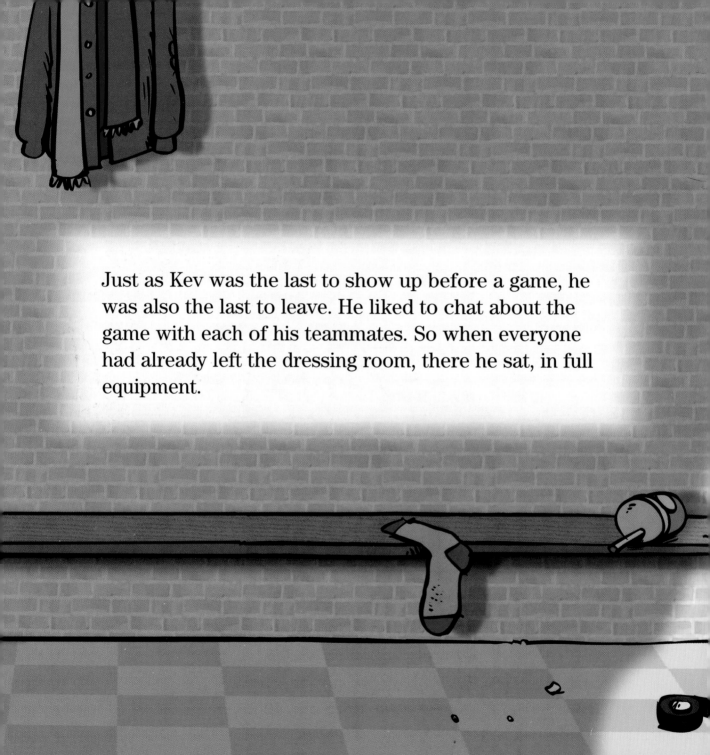

Just as Kev was the last to show up before a game, he was also the last to leave. He liked to chat about the game with each of his teammates. So when everyone had already left the dressing room, there he sat, in full equipment.

At night as he lay in bed, Kev would think about hockey.

Like his friend Brady, he would dream about racing up the ice, sparks flying from his skates, and scoring the winning goal.

Kev never scored the winning goal.
Kev never scored any goals.
Nobody knew that this bothered Kev.
He kept this secret to himself.

One day after practice, the coach sat down next to Kev.

With a proud smile on his face, he said to his player, "Kev, the coach from another team wants to know if you'd like to play for them. They need another center for their top line. I'd hate to lose you, but you'd be getting a ton of ice time. It's your decision, but they need to know by tomorrow."

For the first time in his life, Kev was speechless.

He sat alone in the dressing room to think.

"Could I leave the Icehogs?" Kev said out loud.
But nobody was around to answer him.

Again that night, Kev dreamed about racing up the ice, sparks flying from his skates, and scoring the winning goal.

He was on the top line for his new team. He was one of the stars. This time when he woke up, he realized it didn't have to be a dream.

At the rink the next morning, the Icehogs waited for Kev to come bounding through the door — late as usual. They knew something was going on when it was the coach who walked through the door last, not Kev.

"Icehogs, we may have lost a player today. Kev has been asked to play for the Stars." As he headed toward the door, the coach said with a chuckle, "Make sure you don't pass him the puck!" The Icehogs were stunned. They knew the dressing room wouldn't be the same without Kev.

With his equipment slung over his shoulder, Kev walked slowly down the hallway toward the dressing rooms. He looked first at the Icehogs' door, and then at the Stars' door.

"I can't wait to score a huge goal!" said Kev . . .

and bounded through
the Icehogs' dressing room door!
"I'm **baaack!**" Kev announced, waving his
Icehogs jersey in the air.

Brady and the others cheered,

*"We've got the power,
We've got the might,
Kev likes to chatter,
But he's always polite!"*

Kev took his place beside the refs during warm up, making sure everything was set to go.

As he was escorted over to the bench, his cheering began.

"Let's go team! Play hard! Have fun!"

The Icehogs and the Stars battled hard with the game ending in a tie.

Kev played his best game ever, but it was Brady who was awarded the MVP — the Most Valuable Player.

The teams lined up to shake hands. When Kev got to the end of the line, he turned to shake hands with his teammates. Brady reached out and grabbed Kev's hand.

"You were awesome!" he said to his smiling friend.

"Thanks Brady Brady. I think I was too!" Kev laughed.

Brady's dad tucked him into bed that night. "Great game son. Can I see your MVP puck?"

"Nope. I gave it to Kev. I thought he deserved it more — after all, doesn't MVP stand for Most Vocal Player?" Brady said with a wink, and rolled over to dream about hockey.